DISCARD
Woodbourne Library
Washington-Centerville Public Library
Centerville

P9-ASH-662

A Note to Parents and Caregivers:

Read-it! Readers are for children who are just starting on the amazing road to reading. These beautiful books support both the acquisition of reading skills and the love of books.

 The PURPLE LEVEL presents basic topics and objects using high frequency words and simple language patterns.

 The RED LEVEL presents familiar topics using common words and repeating sentence patterns.

 The BLUE LEVEL presents new ideas using a larger vocabulary and varied sentence structure.

 The YELLOW LEVEL presents more challenging ideas, a broad vocabulary, and wide variety in sentence structure.

 The GREEN LEVEL presents more complex ideas, an extended vocabulary range, and expanded language structures.

 The ORANGE LEVEL presents a wide range of ideas and concepts using challenging vocabulary and complex language structures.

When sharing a book with your child, read in short stretches, pausing often to talk about the pictures. Have your child turn the pages and point to the pictures and familiar words. And be sure to reread favorite stories or parts of stories.

There is no right or wrong way to share books with children. Find time to read with your child, and pass on the legacy of literacy.

Adria F. Klein, Ph.D.
Professor Emeritus
California State University
San Bernardino, California

Editor: Patricia Stockland
Page production: Melissa Kes/JoAnne Nelson/Tracy Davies
Art Director: Keith Griffin
Managing Editor: Catherine Neitge
The illustrations in this book were rendered digitally.

Picture Window Books
5115 Excelsior Boulevard
Suite 232
Minneapolis, MN 55416
877-845-8392
www.picturewindowbooks.com

Copyright © 2005 by Picture Window Books
All rights reserved. No part of this book may be reproduced without written
permission from the publisher. The publisher takes no responsibility for the use of
any of the materials or methods described in this book, nor for the products thereof.

Printed in the United States of America.

Library of Congress Cataloging-in-Publication Data
Jones, Christianne C.
John Henry / by Christianne C. Jones ; illustrated by Ben Peterson.
p. cm. — (Read-it! readers tall tales)
Summary: Retells some of the legends of John Henry, an African-American hero
who raced against a steam drill to lay railroad tracks on a mountain.
ISBN 1-4048-1002-1 (hardcover)
1. John Henry (Legendary character)—Legends. [1. John Henry (Legendary
character)—Legends. 2. African Americans—Folklore. 3. Folklore—United States.]
I. Peterson, Ben, ill. II. Title. III. Series.

PZ8.1.J646Jo 2004
398.2'0973'02—dc22   2004023359

John Henry

By Christianne C. Jones
Illustrated by Ben Peterson

Special thanks to our advisers for their expertise:

Adria F. Klein, Ph.D.
Professor Emeritus, California State University
San Bernardino, California

Susan Kesselring, M.A.
Literacy Educator
Rosemount-Apple Valley-Eagan (Minnesota) School District

PICTURE WINDOW BOOKS
Minneapolis, Minnesota

Bang! Bang! Bang! The hammering began the minute John Henry was born.

Some people say John was born with a hammer in each hand.

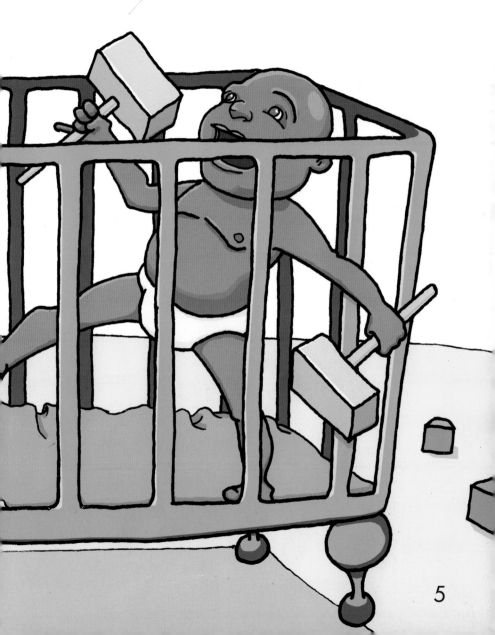

John Henry was a huge baby.

By the time he was two years old, he was bigger than his parents!

He got bigger and bigger every day.
John grew right out of his house!

As he grew up, John banged, clanged, and hammered away.

He hammered everything in sight, even fence posts.

When John Henry turned ten,
his parents sent him to work on
the railroads.

John happily hammered steel from morning to night.

John worked his hammer at lightning speed.

Clank! Clank! Clank! He became the best steel driver in the world.

One day, a man arrived with a machine. It was called a steam drill. The steam drill was a new invention.

The man said the machine was the best steel driver in the world.

The machine was said to work faster

than twelve men!

John Henry said he could work faster than the steam drill.

He challenged the machine to a steel-driving contest.

News of the challenge spread.

Hundreds of people gathered near a mountain to watch John Henry battle the machine.

The day of the challenge was dark and stormy, but nothing slowed down John Henry.

With two huge hammers, he started pounding tracks into the mountain.

Wind howled, and thunder crashed.

Sweat poured off John's face.

John banged and banged until he
out-hammered the machine.

The banging stopped. The crowd cheered loudly. Even the sun came out to celebrate.

John dragged himself from the
mountain and fell to
the ground.

John's great big victory was too much for his great big heart.

John Henry died with a hammer in each hand.

More *Read-it!* Readers

Bright pictures and fun stories help you practice your reading skills. Look for more books at your level.

TALL TALES

Annie Oakley, Sharp Shooter by Eric Blair

John Henry by Christianne C. Jones

Johnny Appleseed by Eric Blair

The Legend of Daniel Boone by Eric Blair

Paul Bunyan by Eric Blair

Pecos Bill by Eric Blair

Looking for a specific title or level? A complete list of *Read-it!* Readers is available on our Web site: *www.picturewindowbooks.com*